FAYETTE
PRESS

To my children, of course.

1

Bored to Tears

One Friday evening, eight-year-old Princess Celeste was in the royal garden playing croquet with her brothers, Prince Jude and Prince Torrin. Perfect pink clouds, like baby dragons, floated in the sky. The weather was warm, but still lovely.

But Princess Celeste was not having a good time at all.

Some children enjoy croquet, which involves smacking brightly painted wooden balls with wooden mallets through little hoops in the yard. But croquet was the only game Princess Celeste was allowed to play. Ever. Besides chess, and did chess even count?

Prince Jude, who was the oldest of the royal children at thirteen, tossed his blue croquet ball on the ground, not bothering to chase it while the ball bumped down a little hill and landed in a royal fishpond. "Croquet is so childish! We must find something else to do."

Prince Torrin, aged eleven, sat on a bench, plucked a twig from a nearby bush and began to pull the leaves from the branches. Sweat dripped from his forehead and splattered his royal pantaloons, making strange splotches on the purple velvet. "I hate croquet," he said fiercely, driving his stick into the ground. "Hate it to death."

"Mama says not to say hate," said Princess Celeste. Taking careful aim, she whacked her orange ball with her orange mallet. The ball went through one hoop, a little dip in the lawn, and hit the center peg in the middle. "There." She yawned. "I've won."

"It's the third game you've won today!" Jude groaned and slumped against a column.

"I HATE croquet!" Torrin yelled. And before his sister or brother could stop him, he stood and flung his mallet at a statue of a very serious man who, for some reason, was perched on a giant marble pinecone.

The mallet clipped the statue on the end of its nose. The nose broke off and dropped to the ground, rolling over and over until it came to a stop at Celeste's gold brocade slippers.

"Ahhh!" she screamed, clutching at the long brown hair that streamed over her shoulders in ringlets. "Torrin, you broke Harold!"

Jude came over to inspect the statue. "Yep. It looks pretty bad. He'll never smell the same again."

A woman in a long brown dress with bell-shaped sleeves ran over the hill. "Children, what have you done! Merciful heavens!"

"The heavens weren't so merciful to Harold," muttered Torrin.

A rather stout man wearing a suit and a shiny black hat came over the hill, after the woman. "Jude, it's time for your Latin lesson." He stopped short at the sight of the de-nosed statue and tapped his clean-shaven chin with pudgy fingers. "Oh dear. Which one of you did this?"

The children stole glances at each other, their lips in three tight lines. They might fuss and fight amongst themselves, but their royal sibling code was simple. They never tattled. Tattling was common and petty, something royals would never do.

The woman took off her long, shawl-like hat, which rather looked like a curtain over a small puppet stage and wiped her brow. "There's no point in asking, Sir Gringle. You'll never get it out of them."

Sir Gringle picked up the statue's nose and tucked it somewhere in the depths of his robes. "We'll have the royal sculptor in to mend it next week. This is the third repair this month, children." He arched an eyebrow and glared at them. "Your parents are meeting with the Duchess of Foresooth today, so we won't bother them with this travesty. I suppose you'll have your normal punishment. Straight to bed, and only barley-water soup for supper."

Jude groaned.

"I hate barley-water soup to death." Torrin muttered. He straightened his shoulders. "Sir Gringle, it was my fault. Jude and Celeste didn't do anything."

"Regardless, you have all disturbed my peace," said Sir Gringle. "Wouldn't you agree, Lady Gertle?"

"To be sure." Lady Gertle's wrinkled lips twitched as she picked up croquet mallets and balls, her sleeves and shawls flapping about her as she moved. "Disturbing the peace is not becoming to royals."

"You'll have fifty additional arithmetic problems to do on Monday, Prince Torrin." Sir Gringle adjusted his spectacles. "And I *should* make it seventy. Prince Torrin?"

Torrin's head was turned away. His eyes were fixed on one of the castle towers. It was the smallest tower, with a tiny window, almost too high to see.

"Prince Torrin, did you not hear Sir Gringle?" demanded Lady Gertle.

"What?" Torrin turned around. "Fifty problems. Got it."

Celeste was mystified. Usually Torrin would argue and moan if he received such a punishment. But he didn't say another word about it as they put away the croquet mallets.

After cleaning up, the three children shuffled through the back door and up the stairs, stopping in front of Jude and Torrin's bedroom door.

Celeste folded her arms. "Torrin, I wish you would stop breaking things. But it was noble of you to tell the truth."

Jude opened the door and looked into the room. "The barley-water soup is already here. I can smell it. Yuck." He slammed the door.

Celeste wrinkled her nose. "Mama wouldn't make us eat it." She sighed. Mama was busy with royal matters. So busy she often had headaches. The three children would never bother her over barley-water soup. Sir Gringle and Lady Gertle knew this. They always found punishments that were bad, but not so terrible the children would tell their parents.

"Well, I suppose I'll go on to bed." Celeste turned to leave.

"Wait. I have an idea!" Torrin smiled, and a special light gleamed in his eyes.

Celeste and Jude knew that light meant two things. Fun and trouble. Torrin was always getting them into adventures.

"What crazy idea do you have in your head tonight?" Jude asked. "Last time we went along with you, we accidentally got locked up in the dungeon and missed afternoon tea."

"Ye-es," said Torrin. "But you have to admit we had a fabulous time. We found those rusty old chains and the poems scratched on the dungeon wall from our great-grandfather's rule." He shrugged. "But suit yourself. You can go eat your old barley-water soup."

"I had fun when we pretended a dragon was chasing us." Celeste leaned forward. "What's your idea?"

"Okay, here goes." Torrin dropped his voice to a whisper. "When we're travelling to the village, do you ever turn to look at our house?"

"Sure," said Jude. "It's pretty grand."

"Especially when it's been newly whitewashed," said Celeste.

"Yeah," said Torrin. "But how many towers does it have?"

Jude tapped his chin and stared up at the ceiling. "Four. It has four."

"And what's in each tower?" Torrin asked.

Celeste counted on her fingers, "The guards keep watch in the east tower, 'cause it's the tallest. The west one is where Papa keeps his fifth library."

"And the third is the smallest, where Mother goes to paint sometimes," put in Jude.

"Yes." Torrin nodded. "But what about the fourth tower? The one we can see from the garden. What do we use that one for?"

The royal siblings stared at each other.

"I haven't the foggiest idea," Jude tapped his chin. "But you're right. I've never gone up there."

"When I was being lectured by Sir Gringle . . . I saw a light in the window," said Torrin.

Jude frowned. "How do you know it wasn't the sunset reflecting on the windowpane?"

"Couldn't have been." Torrin shook his head. "The sun sets behind the castle, remember? Nope. Someone's up there. I think we should find out what's going on. Tonight."

"But where would we even start?" asked Jude. "I don't remember seeing a door or staircase we weren't allowed to use." He paused. "Except for the dungeon now."

Torrin frowned and looked up at the ceiling. "We should search the back corner of the castle. Maybe we never found something because we didn't know to look."

"All right, I'll come along." Jude opened the door to their room, letting out more of the barley-water stench. "Wait for me here."

In a moment he'd returned with a wooden sword in one hand and a dagger in the other. He handed the dagger to Torrin and stuck the sword in his belt-loop.

"These are practice swords," said Torrin. "They can't hurt anyone."

"I know, but at least we'll have something, just in case," said Jude.

"What about me?" asked Celeste. "I need something too."

Jude rubbed the back of his neck. "You can open the door really fast if we have to escape. You'll need both hands empty for that."

"Oh, all right." Celeste didn't like this idea much, but she didn't want to waste any more time arguing. One of the servants could be up to check on them at any moment.

The three children snuck down the rear staircase from the sleeping quarters and in to the wide, long hallway. Only a few remaining candles flickered from alcoves along the corridor since the back part of the castle wasn't used often at this time of night.

"It's dark," said Celeste.

Jude pulled a torch from a slot beside the door. "I'll light this if it gets too bad, but we don't want anyone seeing us."

Torrin walked along the hall, examining the stones in the wall. "I wonder if there's some kind of hidden passage. It's got to be here. Why would someone build a fourth tower with no way to reach it?"

"Decoration?" suggested Celeste.

Torrin gave her a long stare and returned to his search.

Jude lit the torch from one of the candles and held it up to a long tapestry hanging on the wall. "Interesting."

The tapestry was so faded that Celeste could barely make out the pattern. Tiny stitches depicted a countryside. It looked like a map, with miniature castles and mountains and rivers stretched out across a fabric surface.

A green horse pranced along the edge of the tapestry. Celeste touched the velvety nose.

"CREAK." The wall moved beneath the fabric.

Torrin whirled around. "What was that?" He ran to the tapestry, shoving Celeste out of the way.

"Hey, you hurt me," she protested.

"Sorry." Torrin flung back the tapestry and there it was. A door. With a metal handle. He pulled down on the hasp and the door swung open.

"Shall we?" he said.

.

2

The Secret Staircase

Jude held up his torch to reveal a narrow hallway. The three children stepped inside, and Torrin closed the door behind them.

Something scurried in front of Celeste in the darkness. She jumped back. "A rat! How can there be a rat in our castle?"

"It's a big rock house." Jude's face glowed in the torchlight. "Maybe some of the stones fell out of the walls and the rats got in that way."

Celeste crept closer to Jude. "I don't want to explore the tower if it has rats running around."

Torrin turned. "Come on, Celeste." His curly hair stood on end because he'd been running his fingers through it like he always did when he was excited. "You know what will happen if we go back now. We'll lay there in our beds and won't be able to sleep. We'll wonder, and wonder. We might drive ourselves crazy with all that wondering, and we'll never find out what's up in the tower."

"Until Papa retires and I'm king," said Jude. "Then we can go wherever we want. But that's a long time from now. I don't want to wait until then. Do you, Celeste?"

Celeste imagined herself laying in her royal bed, her little nose pointed up at the fluffy purple canopy that hung over it. She scrunched up her face. Yes, she most certainly would wonder. *And it would drive me absolutely crazy.* She squared her shoulders.

"All right, I suppose I'll go a little further."

The passage was narrower here than the main halls of the castle, and the floor was dusty.

"It doesn't look like the maids get in here to clean much," said Celeste.

"Why would they?" asked Torrin. "If no one ever sees it, who will care about the dust?"

Jude held his torch high, and the light bounced on the walls, creating spooky shadows.

Heavy wooden doors lined the sides of the hall.

"Locked," said Torrin, as he tried one.

"I simply must ask the steward about these doors," said Jude, trying the fifth locked hasp in a row. "What could possibly be stored behind them?"

"Jewels?" Celeste suggested.

"Maybe." Torrin pointed ahead to the end of the passage and the biggest door of all. "Oh great. A dead end. If THAT one is locked, then we'll have nothing to do but turn back."

Jude grabbed the hasp and gave it a firm twist. And then it happened . . . the door clicked open.

"Huzzah!" shouted Torrin, which is a princely way of saying "Yay!"

As mentioned before, the passage where the three children were standing was narrow, dark, and dusty. But this new place was even more tight, more shadowy, and the dust was so thick it ran over the top of their royal slippers. The air was musty and smelled like old shoes. But somehow the room felt more open, like a very high ceiling over their heads.

When Jude lifted his torch, Celeste could see why. They were in a sort of rounded chamber, with stone stairs that spiraled up and around them, disappearing into the blackness, dark as a dragon's lair.

"The fourth tower," breathed Celeste. Her knees began to tremble, just a bit. "Oh, Torrin, I don't think this was a good idea. We know how to get here now. Let's just come back in the daylight sometime. Maybe for your birthday. Next year."

"You can go to bed if you want," said Torrin, stepping up on the first step. "Us men are going up. Right, Jude?"

"No, we aren't leaving our sister here by herself. Flesh and blood don't leave each other behind." Jude said firmly. "But Celeste, can't you go just a little further? I really want to see what's up there."

"Jewels," Torrin reminded her.

"Oh, all right. But I get the most sparkly ones."

The three children trooped up the stairs, around and around, higher and higher.

"It's cold in here." Jude said. His voice echoed off the round walls.

Torrin held a finger to his lips. "Be quiet. We don't want anyone to find us."

Celeste pulled the little shawl she was wearing tighter around her shoulders. "I don't think anyone has climbed these stairs in years. I wonder why?"

Torrin halted as they reached the top stair. "There's a door here, just like the other three towers. Oh, I hope there's something exciting! What if there's not? Oh, I can't stand the idea of a boring old room. I just can't stand it!" He covered his face with his hands.

Celeste leaned against the door, but then popped right back up. For she'd heard something through the battered wooden slats. A humming sound.

3

The Batty Aunt

Celeste's heart beat against her ribcage like a heralding drum (the king used to have trumpets, but drums were all the fashion now). The only time something hummed was when someone could supply the voice.

A person had to be in the room.

A person was humming.

Celeste twisted her hands in front of her. She desperately wanted to know what was on the other side of that wall. *But what if it's a monster? Can monsters hum?*

Jude finally stepped forward and knocked three times. He moved back, and so did Torrin and Celeste, for no one wants to be caught listening at someone's door, especially if a stranger lives there.

The humming stopped. Then something made a scraping sound, like a chair being dragged across a wooden floor. The children stared at each other with wide eyes.

Celeste was tempted to run back down the staircase, but she didn't have a torch of her own. *It's awfully dark.*

She paused; her slipper poised above the first step. *Would Mama run away?* Lifting her chin, she turned back to the door. "Mama wouldn't be afraid."

"Of course Mama wouldn't be afraid," Jude scoffed.

The handle jiggled and the door opened. A crack at first, then wider, until they could see part of a wrinkled face, with one bright eye peering at them. It twinkled in the light of Jude's torch. Wisps of gray hair stuck out over the face.

"Children?" The voice was weathered as an old broom, but still pleasant. "What on earth are the three of you doing up here? Shouldn't you be in bed?"

The door opened wider, and an old woman stepped out. At least, she could be called old, though she didn't look like any elderly person the three children had ever seen. She had gray hair twisted up in a poof at the top of her head like a giant dust bunny. She was wrapped from head to toe in a colorful, scarf-like fabric of golds and reds. The ends of the garment fluttered in the drafts, making her look a bit like a giant butterfly. Her face was thin, and must have been quite pretty at one time, though her nose was a bit sharp at the tip.

This remarkable person pulled a watch from somewhere in the depths of her robe. She held the broad face of the timepiece up to the light and nodded. "As I thought. Why on earth are you up this late, Celeste, Jude and Torrin?"

The children stared at her, their mouths all in the shape of 'o's.

"You know our names?" asked Torrin.

"Of course I do," said the old woman.

"Oh right, because we're the royal children." Jude nodded.

"Actually, I'm your great-aunt, Maggie. Or great-great-aunt." The women tipped her head to the side. "I forget which. But come on in. Since you're here you might as well sit a spell before going back down all those stairs."

"Like, a magic spell?" Celeste gasped. *Is Aunt Maggie a witch?*

Aunt Maggie chuckled. "No, no, no, silly. A spell means for a few minutes. I'd like to get to know you a little better."

The three children glanced at each other. Jude shrugged and squeezed through the narrow doorway. Torrin followed, and Celeste darted in behind them before she could be eaten by the darkness nipping at her heels.

The space was small, with rounded sides, as one would expect in a tower room. Shelves full of books, tools, and carvings of strange, slinking creatures, lined the walls. Candles flickered from various posts.

Aunt Maggie bustled around the room, picking up items and setting them down again. "There's only one chair," she waved towards a regal, red-velvet armchair in front of a desk that was covered in papers. "I suppose you'll have to sit on the floor. My bed's up in the rafter room, you see, so there's nowhere else."

"It's quite all right," said Celeste. Her mama had always taught her to be polite in any situation, no matter what. Even if a giant asked permission to eat you, her mother had said, there was always a way to politely decline. Celeste found a clean spot on the floor and sank down, tucking her knees under her chin.

Jude sat beside her, his sword clattering on the floor.

Torrin scowled, then sighed and joined them as well.

Aunt Maggie clasped her hands before her. "What shall we talk about, now that you're here?"

"Who are you really?" Torrin folded his arms. "I would think if you're truly our aunt, Papa would have told us about you, especially since you live in our house."

"Yes, you would suppose." Aunt Maggie pursed her lips. "Your parents asked me to come live here a long time ago. I'm an inventor and a scientist, so for years I've worked on projects that required absolute peace and quiet. They don't bother with me." She tapped her chin. "I'm not sure they remember I'm here."

"Well, if we're disturbing you, we'll leave." Jude shifted in his spot on the floor, and the wadded-up papers that surrounded him crinkled.

Putting a wrinkled hand on his shoulder, Aunt Maggie shook her head. "No, dear, I'm glad you've come. I've had enough peace and quiet. What I need is a great big noisy fuss, and I think you children are the right people to make it happen."

A bell hanging from the wall suddenly tinkled. Aunt Maggie jumped to her feet, her colorful shawl jumbling itself until Celeste thought she might very well get tangled up and fall, but somehow it furled out again.

"Here we are." Their aunt opened what looked like a small cupboard door. "I'm sure you are hungry, most children are famished nearly all of the time, aren't they? Would you like some tea?"

Celeste gazed around the room. No stove or kitchen was to be seen. A roughly hewn staircase led up to a platform above them. *That must go to her sleeping loft. Could the kitchen be up there?*

Torrin pointed to a jumble of clear tubes and jars on a counter in the corner. "Is that where you make your tea?"

"Make my tea?" Aunt Maggie laughed, pearly teeth flashing in the light of the candles. "Why, child, when would I possibly have time for that? My mind is scientific. I have no room for recipes and cooking methods!"

"Do you use magic?" Jude perked up and craned his neck.

"What is it with you children and magic? Magic doesn't work in this kingdom." Aunt Maggie pulled open the little door to reveal a teapot with steam coming from the spout. A plate, heaped with little cakes, sat beside it.

"Why, those look like cakes from our very own cook! And I know the teapot is from the set downstairs," said Celeste.

"Of course they are." Aunt Maggie passed the plate around. "Your parents may not remember me, but I'm good friends with the cook. Though she sends up enough food for the entire castle. I usually return most of it.

She'll wonder why my appetite is so big tonight. Of course, Lester's here, and he's awfully fond of cakes."

"Is Lester our uncle?" Torrin spoke with his mouth full. Crumbs sprayed across the room in a manner most unbecoming to a young royal.

Aunt Maggie's cheeks reddened, and she laughed. "Gracious me! No, I'm not married. Lester is . . . well, let me see if he'll come down." She leaned back and yelled up to her sleeping bunk. "Lester, come meet the three royal children!"

Celeste peered up at the ceiling, which shone blue and white in the candlelight, with painted golden dragons flying about.

Suddenly, a fuzzy shape hurled out from behind a bookshelf. Celeste screamed and grabbed Jude's practice sword from the floor beside him. She held it up, her hands shaking.

"It's all right, Celeste," said Aunt Maggie. "He won't hurt you."

The animal (which Celeste realized was a bat,) flew down beside Aunt Maggie and settled on the chair's arm.

The bat's leathery wings folded into themselves like Celeste's paper fans. It gazed at her with bright eyes over a sharp, upturned nose.

Celeste put the sword down warily. *Will he really not hurt me?*

"Everything's all right, Lester." Aunt Maggie handed him a bite of cake. "Meet my niece and two nephews."

"I know who they are," Lester said in a furry voice, almost what you would sound like if you were talking with an earmuff in your mouth. "I fly around the castle wherever I please, so I see everything." He studied the children. "These three are usually in bed, asleep, when I see 'em."

Celeste's mouth dropped open. *A talking bat?*

Jude wiped a few crumbs from his mouth. "So, you have a talking bat." He reached for another cake.

"You can talk to Lester directly. He can understand you fine." Aunt Maggie patted Lester's wing.

"How did you learn to talk, uh, Lester?" asked Celeste.

"The wise gnomes of Tolmey." Lester shot out a claw and, before Torrin could do anything, grabbed a chunk of his cake. "They'll teach any animal to talk, but many beasts aren't willing to go into the dark caverns. Most animals want to be out in the nasty hot sun all day." He shook his head. "Not me. Hurts my eyes."

"I always wondered, how do bats fly at night?" asked Jude.

A strange clicking noise sounded through the air. It filled Celeste's head and buzzed in her ears.

"What is that?" She stared at Lester. "Did you make that noise?"

The bat's nose wrinkled, and his lips turned up into a grin. "Yep. When I make that sound, it bounces off of things so I don't run into stuff."

"Well, that's pretty cool." Torrin had a look on his face Celeste recognized. It was how he looked when he was impressed but trying to pretend like he wasn't.

The children remembered their manners enough to wipe their mouths with the napkins presented by Aunt Maggie. The cook sent up plenty of cakes, but they hadn't eaten supper, not even the barley soup. They stared at the empty platter forlornly.

Aunt Maggie clapped her hands. "Children, you'd better leave for tonight. But please come to see me soon. Earlier in the day, perhaps, so you won't have to hurry on to bed. And let your parents know where you are so they won't be worried."

4

An Invitation

The next morning, Celeste awoke in her bedchamber, staring up at the purple velvet canopy covering her bed.

Two wonderful thoughts floated up in her mind. The first was that it was Saturday. Which meant they had no lessons that morning.

The next was the memory of what had happened the night before. She rose from her bed and pulled on her clothes. "It must have been a dream," she said to her reflection in the mirror as she brushed her tresses (tresses is a princessy name for hair). "Talking bats, secret aunts.

It can't be real." She placed her silver hairbrush on a tray and jumped up to go and find her brothers.

She was almost out the door when something tapped on her windowpane.

Her windows were so high she had to stand on a chair to reach the drapes. She pulled them back, and sun blazed into her room.

A large, dark creature was perched on the window's ledge.

Celeste screamed, jumped off the chair, and hid behind her wardrobe. *Is it a gryphon?* Her stomach twisted. Gryphons where fearsome half-lion half-eagle monsters. They lived north of the kingdom and only bothered remote villages, not castles.

The creature tapped again, and Celeste's curiosity outweighed her fear. She crept to the window and turned a little crank on the side. The glass panel swung open.

"Lester, you're real," she breathed.

"Of course, I'm real," said Lester, scowling, if bats can scowl. One of his little bat feet clutched a rolled-up scroll, and he held it out to her. "Maggie wanted me to deliver this, so hurry up and take it. I need some shut eye. Not good for bats to be out at this hour."

Celeste took the scroll. "Thank you very much for delivering our message. Can I do anything else for you?"

The bat looked over her shoulder. "You got any cakes in there? For breakfast, perhaps?"

Celeste checked the tray that had been brought in while she was still sleeping. Her shoulders sagged. "No, just some dry toast. I guess we're still being punished for breaking Harold."

"More's the pity." Lester stretched his leathery wings and flapped away.

"Okay. Bye, Lester." Celeste waved, all the while realizing the absurdity of the situation. *Should a princess talk to a bat?*

She ran down the hall to the royal bedchamber her brothers shared and banged on their door. "Jude, Torrin, wake up!"

Jude opened the door, looking sleepy and still wearing his pajamas. "What?"

Torrin joined him. "Yes, why are you bothering us this early? On a Saturday!"

"Don't be grouchy." Celeste held out the curled-up piece of parchment Lester had given her.

"What do you have there?" Torrin's eyes narrowed into little suspicious slits.

"Lester, the bat, delivered it to my window," Celeste replied.

Jude's eyes widened. "I thought that was a dream."

"Nope."

Torrin snatched the scroll and opened it. "It says, 'Come up to the tower tonight at 8 o'clock sharp if you want to go on an adventure. Bring traveling clothes and make sure to tell your parents you're going on a trip with me.'"

"Oh." Jude groaned. "Mama and Papa never allow us to go anywhere."

Celeste folded her arms. "You mean Sir Gringle and Lady Gertle don't let us go anywhere. They always say not to bother our parents because they're so busy. I think we should try asking Mama and Papa first."

Torrin crumpled up the parchment and threw it at the wall. "We can try. But don't get your hopes up."

Celeste was given the job of asking the king's permission, since she was a daddy's girl.

The king was sorting through royal edicts in the throne room.

Celeste's heart hammered in her chest as she approached the throne, and she swallowed hard. "Papa?"

The king looked over the paper in his hand, a glimpse of a smile tugging on the corner of his mouth. "Yes, my sweetheart. How is your day going?"

"Good. Um. We met our aunt. In the tower."

The king picked up another paper and pulled his spectacles farther down his nose to study it. "Ah yes. How is the old dear?"

"She's fine. But she wanted us to go somewhere with her tonight. I don't know where. It's crazy–"

"Quite good, quite good." The king nodded as he dripped a candle over an envelope and stamped it with a royal seal. The sweet smell of warm beeswax filled the air. "Tell her I said hello."

Celeste gasped. "You mean, you're okay with us going?"

"Of course, of course." The king waved his hand. "My little dove-child, I love you, really I do, but I must get these edicts finished by supper time, or the royal secretary will have my head."

Celeste giggled at the thought of the secretary ordering any such thing. She ran up the stairs, hugging herself with excitement.

Torrin had similar good news. "I was worried we'd get scolded for bothering Aunt Maggie, but Mama said we could go. Didn't even blink an eye."

"Papa said yes, too," said Celeste.

The three children grabbed hands and skipped around in a circle, until Jude frowned and stopped. "I'm much too old for dancing around like this. Aunt Maggie said to prepare, so we should get our things together."

He pulled out the pocket watch he'd been given for his twelfth birthday. "7:30. We'd better get ready." He disappeared into his room and closed the door.

Torrin's eyebrows scrunched together. "I hate when he gets all grown-up like that. He's every bit as excited as we are. And what exactly is he talking about? Where could Aunt Maggie possibly be going? The village? There's nothing to really prepare for. We've been there dozens of times."

"Oh. I hadn't thought of that." The anticipation that had sprung up in Celeste's heart withered just a little. The village was a terribly boring place. Several homes clumped around a bakery, a school, a few churches, and the market. The rare times they'd visited were during the king's speeches or on special days. They hadn't been allowed to talk or play with the local children.

The bigger cities were all much farther away. *Surely Aunt Maggie won't take us to any of those.*

Celeste sighed. At least Lester might come, and any adventure with a talking bat would have to be more exciting.

Jude emerged from his bedroom with a battered hat he must have found at the bottom of the wardrobe on his head. A seldom used knapsack hung on his back, bulging with mysterious lumps. "I decided not to bring the swords this time," he said.

Torrin's lips twitched, and Celeste could tell he was dying to ask what their brother packed, but he didn't say anything.

They headed down the back staircase, Jude with his pack, Celeste with a small satchel containing a few biscuits she'd kept from lunch and an extra dress in case she fell in a pond somehow, and Torrin swinging his empty hands in a nonchalant manner. They ambled through the back castle hall, each lost in their own musings about the trip, until they had almost reached the tapestry covering the secret entrance.

Voices echoed through the hallway.

"Where have those children gone to now?"

"I don't know. I haven't seen them since that disgraceful business with the statue yesterday."

"Cook knew about the barley-water soup for supper, right?"

"Of course, but sometimes that woman gets soft."

"It's Gringle and Gertle!" Jude hissed.

"Hurry up and get in here!" Torrin rushed to the tapestry, yanked it back and tugged on the handle of the secret door. "Oh no! It's stuck!"

The footsteps grew louder. The three children pulled on the hasp until their fingers ached and their faces grew red.

"They'll never allow us to go." Celeste whispered fiercely. "Even if we say Mama and Papa said yes, they'll never let us."

"Try again, together." Jude gestured to the door.

They tugged again, with all of their might.

Suddenly the door swung open and they fell inside the tunnel, in a heap. The tapestry flapped shut behind them, and none too soon.

They righted themselves just as Lady Gertle and Sir Gringle stopped outside the tapestry. Celeste could see the bottom of Gertle's practical brown slippers through the crack below the door.

"I could have sworn I heard scuffling in here," said Sir. Gringle.

"Likewise," said Lady Gertle. "Oh, those children will be the death of me!"

"They'll turn up, eventually," said Sir Gringle. "Tonight we'll give them cabbage soup."

Torrin made a face in the semi-darkness.

"I'll inform the king of their disappearance," said Lady Gertle.

"Let's not be too hasty," Sir Gringle's voice became crafty. "We'll carry on a search of our own first. The children are always getting lost, I think we should let them find their own way back for once. Maybe they'll learn a lesson."

The children held their breath as Lady Gertle and Sir Gringle talked. It seemed like they would never leave, but finally they did.

Jude softly closed the door. "Now, on to Aunt Maggie."

5

On the Way

Aunt Maggie opened the door. Her cheeks were pink and she wore a hat similar to Jude's, but not quite as battered. Little wisps of hair floated around her wrinkled, smiling face.

"Ah, children, you came! There's not a moment to lose. Torrin, my dear, please grab that package there." She pointed to a large woven basket covered with a red-checked cloth.

Torrin lifted the basket. "Whew. It's heavy, but it sure smells good, Aunt Maggie. Where are we going, anyway?"

Aunt Maggie put on a pair of giant spectacles and blinked at him. "Didn't I say in the note? We're going to Rellyland."

"Rellyland?" Jude squinted at her. "I'm in my third year of kingdom maps and I've never heard of that place. Is it far?"

"Far? Not really. If you have practical transportation. Which no one else around here does." Aunt Maggie grabbed a bag and slung it over her shoulder. She looked them up and down. "You're all dressed fine, and those shoes will do nicely, Celeste. Good for climbing over boulders and slogging through swamps if need be. Follow me, children."

She pushed a curtain aside to reveal a little wooden door, barely large enough for her to squeeze through with all the sacks and bags. Jude and Torrin pushed in after.

Celeste followed last, heart bursting with excitement.

The door led to a narrow staircase, much smaller than any they'd seen in the castle. Aunt Maggie beckoned to them. "Come children. It's a little dark and steep, so be careful."

Lester flapped above them, humming to himself in a muffled way.

After climbing a few stairs they reached another door. Fortunately, this one swung outwardly, otherwise they might not have been able to get it open, with so many people crammed into the small space. They stepped out into the cool evening.

"Why, we're on the roof!" said Jude. "Why are we up here, Aunt Maggie? Shouldn't we be in the stables? Haven't the grooms prepared horses for us? Or a wagon?"

"Surely we'll be taking the second-best carriage," said Celeste.

"Goodness, no," Aunt Maggie scoffed. "We'd never get to the kingdom of Rellyland in the carriage. At least," she tapped her chin, "not for a good long while." She went to a very large, tarp-covered object in the center of the tower's roof.

Aunt Maggie tugged on the tarp. "Help me with this."

Jude, Torrin, and Celeste each grabbed a corner of the tarp and pulled. After a bit of crackling and creaking, the tarp came off in a swoop. Underneath was a strange machine.

It wasn't a wagon, or a carriage. In fact it didn't look like any traveling device Celeste had seen. It was wider than her royal bedchamber, with two flat, flapping, arm-like stalks on either side.

Celeste stared at it. *It almost looks like Lester. Or his shape, anyway.*

Hinges joined the arms in the middle.

Jude pointed to the flat arms. "Maybe they flap up and down," he whispered to Celeste. "Perhaps the thing flies? But why does it have wheels too?"

The contraption did have two wheels on the bottom.

Below the big, flat arms, hanging from the frame, were two gigantic baskets, each large enough to hold a couple of people.

In the very center was a small chair and a set of pedals with gears and pulleys that ran to the flaps.

"What do you call this thing, Aunt Maggie?" said Torrin.

"It's my Windlesoar," said Aunt Maggie as she bustled around, checking ropes and levers and kicking the wheels. "I invented it myself. Give me another few minutes. I have to make sure everything's in perfect condition so we won't have any problems. Rellyland is quite a journey."

Celeste wrinkled her nose. "Won't Mama and Papa worry about us if we don't come back tonight?"

Lester flew to the Windlesoar and grabbed the framework with his claws, hanging upside down. "Don't worry about them. We took care of that."

"We're all good to go." Aunt Maggie flipped up the lid

to one of the baskets and pointed inside. "Celeste, you and Torrin will sit in this basket. Jude, you and Lester may ride in the other one along with the supplies. It's important that everything balances out."

Celeste's mouth dropped open. "We're going to ride in the baskets? Are we going to trundle along the ground? Won't that be bumpy?" Her bones ached at the thought.

"Didn't I tell you, child?" said Aunt Maggie. "We're flying through the air. Like Lester."

Jude frowned. "What if we fall?"

Aunt Maggie patted the Windlesoar's seat. "I haven't had an accident yet. We'd only be in trouble if we hit a storm, and there shouldn't be any rain for days. Don't worry, children, your parents would never have let you come if they thought you would be in danger." She clasped her hands together. "We're going to have so much fun!"

Torrin and Celeste looked at Jude. He was the older brother, and though they would never admit it, they trusted his judgment.

Jude slowly nodded. "I suppose we'll be all right."

They climbed into the baskets as Aunt Maggie instructed.

Wide, comfortable seats had been built into the sides of the baskets. Even though Torrin sat across from Celeste, she didn't feel a bit squished. She wondered how things were going with Jude and Lester. She peeked over the edge of the basket.

Aunt Maggie climbed on the chair in the middle and put her feet on the pedals. She began to push them, her legs whirling around in a blur.

Celeste sat back down as the flat objects on the sides began to move up and down, just like Jude had suggested. "Why, they're like bat wings," Celeste said to Torrin.

His mouth moved, but she didn't hear his reply because the wings grew louder.

The wheels on either side of the contraption began to turn. Celeste realized they were on some sort of upward-sloping ramp. Slowly the contraption made its way up. Faster and faster the wheels turned. Faster and faster the wings moved.

"We're coming to the end of the ramp!" cried Torrin. "We're going to fall off the side of the castle and be smashed to bits!"

Suddenly, they were in the middle of the air, with nothing around them.

Celeste closed her eyes, and her throat stung with fear. A horrible crash would come, any second now. But it never did. Instead she had a curious feeling of being lifted, like when she was smaller and her papa would pick her up and swing her around.

Could it be? She opened her eyes and stared at Torrin who was staring back at her. The basket swung gently from side to side. She gripped the rim of the basket and peeked over the edge. Torrin did the same thing on his side of the basket. The giant wings moved above them. It was true! They were flying!

I wonder how Jude is doing now? I hope he doesn't get sick. She didn't feel queasy at all. *How long will we be up in the air? Perhaps we can stop after a while and Jude can take over pedaling. He's pretty strong.* For some reason, this thought comforted her, and after a few moments of peaceful swaying she fell asleep.

6

A Night in the Woods

She awoke to Torrin shouting at her.

"Celeste, we landed. It was quite a bump! I can't believe you didn't wake up."

She yawned. "I was having a dream. We were in a land of candy and bonbons with no barley-water soup anywhere in sight."

Torrin grinned. "That sounds great! I wonder if they have sweets in the village we're going to."

"Aunt Maggie's basket of food smelled nice," said Celeste. "Maybe we stopped because it's time to eat."

"I sure hope so." Torrin rubbed his stomach.

Celeste rose to her feet, her legs a bit trembly. She peeked over the rim of the basket. Everything was dark except for a glowing light that bobbed a few feet away. "Are you out there, Aunt Maggie?"

The light came toward them. Jude's face glimmered under a torch. "Come on out. Aunt Maggie made a fire and supper's all ready. We're staying here for the night."

"Is there an inn?" Suddenly Celeste missed her comfy canopy bed. She wiggled her toes inside her walking shoes. How would she sleep without her royal fuzzy bed slippers?

Jude helped Celeste and Torrin out of the basket and they followed close to his torch, keeping watch for rocks and bushes and other things that might trip them up.

Hope there's no snakes. Celeste's skin crawled at the thought.

Fortunately, the fire was close. What looked like a lumpy rock rose as they approached. It was Aunt Maggie, wrapped in a gray blanket.

The delicious scent of frying meat filled the air.

Aunt Maggie said, "Come children, you must be hungry after that long journey."

Celeste, Torrin and Jude sat down on smooth rocks that circled the campfire.

Questions bubbled up inside of Celeste, but nothing was more powerful than her rumbling stomach, so she decided to wait until after dinner before asking anything.

Aunt Maggie passed around wooden plates with food. There was ham, biscuits, and green beans.

"Did our cook send this food with us?" asked Celeste.

"Of course," said Aunt Maggie. "Like I said before, I don't cook if I don't have to. I just warmed it up."

"Where are the people we're going to meet?" asked Jude after he emptied his platter.

"We haven't arrived in Rellyland yet," said Aunt Maggie as she gathered up the plates. She handed around cookies, much to the children's delight. "We'll finish our journey tomorrow. It isn't far from here but I 'm weary and we all need rest."

"But Aunt Maggie, where will we sleep?" Celeste asked.

Jude waved his hand. "Didn't you see, Celeste?"

Celeste whirled around. Behind them were two silken tents made of gold and red material. Each tent seemed big enough to hold a carriage, horses and all.

"One is for the boys, and one is for you and me, Celeste." Aunt Maggie scraped the plates out into the bushes and stacked them together.

Despite her nap in the air, Celeste suddenly felt exhausted. She stood, brushing the cookie crumbs from her lap. "It feels strange not washing up before bed."

Aunt Maggie handed each of the three children a small bag. "I brought you bedtime supplies. Go on down to the stream. It's a bit cold but it'll do. And take these plates to clean up while you're at it."

"Clean plates? Like a servant?" Torrin folded his arms.

"You're on an adventure now," Aunt Maggie said. "Adventurers all pitch in when a job needs to be done, and I expect nothing less from you."

"Oh, all right." Torrin picked up the stack of plates and headed down to the stream, with Jude and Celeste following.

The brook ran over a jumble of rocks, glistening in the moonlight. It wasn't very wide. Celeste figured she could jump across it if she tried. Willow trees hung down from the banks in knotted tangles, along with twisted ropes of grapevine.

"It's a little bit creepy down here." Celeste wondered how many eyes were watching them from the trees.

"But isn't it exciting?" Jude's eyes shone in the light of the torch. "We're seeing a place that maybe even Mama and Papa haven't been."

"You think so? I thought they'd travelled to every part of the kingdom." Torrin knelt by the water's edge and swished his toothbrush around in the water–yes, they had toothbrushes and toothpaste in those days. He squirted a small amount of toothpaste onto his brush but stopped before it reached his mouth.

His eyes widened. "What is that?" he whispered.

Celeste and Jude followed his gaze.

A faint pink light flickered on the riverbank, then disappeared. Then another one, this time blue, and then a green one.

Goosebumps pricked Celeste's arms and she didn't dare to move.

Aunt Maggie crashed through the trees to the riverbank. "Children, what's taking so long down here?"

"Shh," Jude hissed. "Something's out there!"

Aunt Maggie peered at the side of the river where they were all staring. "Oh," she chuckled. "That's nothing to be afraid of. Those are just the glowmies."

"Glowmies? I never learned about those in biology or zoology," said Jude.

"I'm beginning to wonder if Sir Gringle knows as much about the world as he thinks," Torrin muttered.

"You're about to learn a lot of things that weren't in your schoolbooks." Aunt Maggie gave a knowing smile.

One of the glowing lights hovered closer until it was only a few feet away from Celeste. The creature's body was shaped like a butterfly, but was the size of a large bird, with iridescent glowing wings. The light it gave was too bright for her to see its little face. The glowmie giggled at her and flew away.

"How beautiful," she breathed.

"Yes," said Aunt Maggie. "But don't let them see you eating, or they'll snatch the food right out of your hands. Especially cookies."

"Good thing I ate the last one," said Torrin.

Dozens of glowmies fluttered around them as they headed back to the tents.

Celeste asked, "Aunt Maggie, how come these places and creatures aren't in our lessons? Or even the books in the castle library?"

Aunt Maggie shrugged. "I suppose kings and queens from the past didn't want children going on adventures like this by themselves. Even though the glowmies are beautiful and harmless, plenty of other things in these woods could hurt you if you don't use the right precautions."

"Do we have the right precautions?" asked Jude.

"Of course we do," said Aunt Maggie. "I sprinkled repellent all around the camp area first thing when we landed. My own special blend, guaranteed to keep away creepers and their closest cousins, cloppers." Celeste and Torrin looked at each other with open mouths.

Celeste was too afraid to ask what a creeper or a clopper was.

Celeste followed Aunt Maggie into the brightly colored tent. Two thick bedrolls had been arranged on either side of the space, piled with comfy-looking blankets and pillows. Celeste couldn't imagine how Aunt Maggie had fit all of those things into the baskets, but she was learning her questions weren't always rewarded with satisfying answers.

Celeste snuggled deep into the soft blankets, a delightful warmth spreading through her. When she closed her eyes, she could still see the colored lights of the glowmies. Her mind blazed with wonder. *What amazing things will we see tomorrow?*

7

Rellyland

As often happens when one is sleeping, it seemed like only a few moments had passed before Aunt Maggie shook Celeste awake. Really, it must have been much longer than that, because the first light of dawn was peeking over the ridge of trees when Celeste stepped outside the tent. She didn't feel one bit stiff, but refreshed and ready for new adventures.

Jude and Torrin were already at the campfire. The sound of sizzling sausages filled the air.

"Celeste, you've got to try one of these," said Torrin, holding up a skewered sausage. "I've already had three."

"Don't eat too many." Aunt Maggie tossed a few more sticks into the fire. "We still have a ways to fly and we have to keep the baskets balanced."

"Does it make a difference if it's inside or outside of my stomach?" Torrin asked as he put another sausage on his plate.

"Good point," said Aunt Maggie. "Now you're thinking scientifically."

Sir Gringle would have scolded us for arguing, Celeste thought as she ate one of the delicious sausages. *Of course, Sir Gringle would never have taken us camping in the first place.* She giggled at the thought.

The children helped Maggie put out the campfire and pick everything up. Amazingly, the tents folded down to packets that could fit in a pocket. Some of the items were stored in compartments within the basket seats, while others hung from bags on the sides. In no time at all, they'd cleaned up the campsite.

The children climbed into their baskets.

As the Windlesoar rose into the air once more, Celeste's head buzzed with wondering. *What will Rellyland be like? What will we see?* To think that only two nights before they were playing boring old croquet in the garden when Aunt Maggie had been up in the tower the entire time!

Torrin tapped his foot against the side of the basket, something he always did when he was excited and impatient. "How long do you think it will take us to get to where we're going?"

"I don't know." Celeste propped her chin on her hands. "But I bet it'll be wonderful."

"I want to see what's happening." Torrin stood on his bench and looked over the edge of the basket. "Wow, Celeste, check this out! You can see for miles!"

"Are you sure it's safe?"

"Aunt Maggie didn't say not to," Torrin replied.

"That's true, she didn't." Celeste couldn't contain her curiosity anymore. She climbed on her basket seat and joined Torrin. The countryside spread out before them like the tapestry on the castle wall, except the colors weren't dingy and dulled from dust. Rivers sparkled in the sunlight. Trees of every shade of green waved gently beneath them.

"Look down there, in the field!" Torrin shouted.

A large number of animals grazed below them. They were like horses, but Celeste had never seen horses like that. Most of the steeds in her papa's stable were brown and black. One very fine stallion was pure white. Her papa had paid a bag of gold for him.

These horses were dark blue and purple, with silver or golden manes and tails. A little green foal ran across the field, kicking up his heels. As he ran, showers of sparks flew behind him.

"Wow!" Celeste and Torrin exclaimed together.

"Just like the horse on the tapestry," said Celeste. As a princess, she'd seen lovely gowns, precious jewels, and all sorts of other treasures. But she'd never seen anything as beautiful as that little foal. She knew she'd never forget the sight, even when she was as old as Aunt Maggie.

"Though she's not really that old," she whispered to herself. The sparkle in her eye was quite young. Maybe even younger than Celeste.

She didn't have much longer to think about the foal, because the flying contraption swooped lower. Down, down; until it seemed like the ground was rushing up to meet them. Celeste screamed and curled up in the bottom of the basket.

"We were fine last time," Torrin scoffed. "Don't be such a baby."

As Torrin said, the Windlesoar landed with a far gentler thump than Celeste was expecting.

"Children, come out. We've arrived in Rellyland!" said Aunt Maggie.

Celeste and Torrin climbed out of their basket, while across from them Jude did the same.

Jude rushed over to them, a huge smile covering his face. "Did you see those horses? That big red one was something, wasn't he?"

"I liked the blue one," said Torrin. "I wonder if we could bring a team of grooms here from the livery stable and capture one."

Celeste rolled her eyes. "It's just like you boys. Those horses looked happy the way they were. Wild and free."

Jude folded his arms. "I guess you're right."

"I don't know how we'd get them home anyway," said Torrin. "It's not like they'd fit in a basket."

Celeste moved a few steps away from the basket to take in her surroundings.

The Windlesoar had landed in a grassy cove, surrounded on three sides by tall cliffs. A wide river rushed past them a short distance away.

The grass beneath Celeste's feet looked so fine and soft that she longed to remove her shoes and feel it between her toes.

Strange trees grew all around them. Their branches were filled with round fruit, a little larger than cherries, hanging from the stems. Suddenly, it seemed a very long time since breakfast. Celeste's mouth watered.

As though Aunt Maggie could read her thoughts, she went over to a tree and plucked a large handful of berries. "Here you are, children. These are candoberries."

Each child popped a berry in their mouth, and immediately smiled. The candoberries tasted like lemon pie, the perfect blend of sour and sweet.

Lester popped out of Jude's basket, wearing a frown on his fuzzy face. His eyes were barely open in thin glittery slits. He regarded the landing place without a word and disappeared back into the basket.

"Don't forget, he's not a morning person," Aunt Maggie muttered to Celeste. She went to the basket and pulled out a tarp. "Children, help me cover the Windlesoar. I don't want a wandering glome to come by and take a fancy to it."

"But can't they just remove the tarp?" asked Jude as the children spread the covering over the craft.

"They could, but they'd have to spot it first." Aunt Maggie tucked in the final corner of canvas.

Celeste blinked. "Why, I can't even see it anymore!"

"Nope. It's an invisibility tarp, given to me by the Gilder of Gilmore." Aunt Maggie dusted her hands on her skirt.

"But how will *we* find it again?" Celeste whispered to Torrin.

"How should I know?" Torrin whispered back. "Aunt Maggie's seemed to know what she's doing so far, don't you think?"

Celeste had to admit this was true.

They set off down a thin path worn through the grass. Lester hung from a rope on Aunt Maggie's back, upside down as most bats would be, his wings folded all around him. He looked for all the word like an old leather satchel.

The air was pleasant and seemed just a bit cooler than the castle gardens. Celeste found her shawl in her pack and threw it around her shoulders.

After meandering a few paces, the small party trooped across a wooden footbridge in single file. All sorts of interesting faces and creatures had been carved in the railings. The children moved slowly, running their fingers over the smooth shapes.

"Don't dawdle," said Aunt Maggie in a kind tone. "We are expected."

"By who?" asked Torrin.

"You mean, by whom," Jude corrected him.

Torrin sighed and rolled his eyes.

"Didn't I tell you? The Eep people requested our presence," said Aunt Maggie. "We're almost there. In fact, the village is just beyond that ridge."

After making their way through the trunks of several fruit trees, they entered a wide meadow filled with the same soft grass.

"What are those?" Torrin pointed to dozens of pole-like structures jutting from the grass, with what appeared to be little boxes perched on the top.

"Almost like mushrooms," murmured Celeste.

"Maybe the biggest mushrooms in the world," Jude muttered back.

The shortest pole came to Celeste's waist while the tallest one towered high over Jude's head.

As she approached the structures, Celeste caught sight of small, pipe-like things on the tops. Out of these pipes puffed clouds of smoke.

"Why–they're chimneys. And those must be homes," said Celeste. But these houses weren't big enough for people. *Unless the people were the size of squirrels?*

The structures were arranged in sort of a circle around the clearing. As Celeste passed each one, she looked as hard as her eyes could stare.

Small wagons, the size of the toys Celeste played with when she was little, dotted the ground. A doll-sized well was in the very center of the clearing, with a doll-sized pail hanging from the rope. Tiny gardens surrounded by miniature fences dotted the ground like green and brown quilt patches.

"Do you think that–elves live here?" whispered Torrin.

"Elves don't exist," Jude whispered back.

"Neither do blue horses," Torrin said in a louder voice.

Aunt Maggie held up her hand. "Magistrate Witherspoon," she said in a loud voice. "You asked for our help. So here we are. Please show yourself."

8

The Eep People

Celeste waited, holding her breath for fear of scaring the unknown inhabitants of the village.

Scuffling sounds came from the houses on the poles, and from the surrounding trees. Little people jumped down from the houses and crept out from behind miniature haystacks and barns.

Like the other creatures in Rellyland, these people were different from any other beings Celeste had ever seen. The tallest man wasn't more than a foot high, while the children were only a few inches. They all had long, thin legs, and rather looked as though they were walking on stilts. All the women wore broad-brimmed hats with long streamers, and everyone sported brightly colored clothes decorated with polka dots.

Celeste fought the urge to hide behind Aunt Maggie. *They're so different.* Beside her, Jude and Torrin's shoulders stiffened.

"Children, do not be alarmed." Aunt Maggie gestured to the people. "These fine folks are the Eeps."

A little man in a top hat and a rather dashing purple suit with white spots strode up to Aunt Maggie and gave a little bow. "Your Excellency, you have come to us again. We are honored by your presence." He gestured to a woman and two Eep children who stood beside him. "You remember my wife, Sally Witherspoon. And my children, Lemon and Huxley."

Huxley seemed to be slightly older than Jude, though the difference in size made it hard to tell. And Lemon might have been Celeste's age. She clutched a stuffed doll and gave Celeste a shy smile.

Sally Witherspoon curtsied. "It's good to see you again, Duchess Margarite."

The royal children stared at each other.

Could she mean Aunt Maggie? Of course she would be a duchess if she's in the royal family. Why didn't I think of that? Celeste shook her head.

Aunt Maggie returned the bow. "Of course, Mrs. Witherspoon. When Lester informed me of your distress, I came as quickly as possible. These are my nephews, Prince Jude and Prince Torrin, and my niece, Princess Celeste. I brought them along to help."

Jude and Torrin made sweeping bows.

Celeste gave a dazzling curtsey despite her travelling dress. *Mama would be proud if she could see us. If there's anything we know how to do, it's bow.*

Magistrate Witherspoon beamed. "Children, thank you for coming to us in our time of need."

Aunt Maggie waved and smiled at the people around them. Several dozen men, women and children had appeared by now and were flocking around her knees like multi-colored ducks. "Everything seems to be fine. Why did you need me to come?"

Magistrate Witherspoon's smile clouded over. "I'm afraid all is not as it appears, Duchess. But you all must be hungry after your long journey. Why don't you come and have lunch with us? We'll discuss our problems then. Troubles never seem so bad on full stomachs."

How will they have enough food to feed us? Celeste followed the crowd through the village. *We're giants to them.*

Her fears were unfounded. Behind the cluster of dwellings was a long wide rock which served as a table, full of steaming dishes and platters piled with food. Though small, the dishes were plentiful.

"The entire village must have pitched in to make this for us," Jude whispered to Torrin and Celeste. "We must eat everything that is given and be thankful."

Torrin scowled. "Of course. Do you think I'm a vagrant?" he whispered fiercely. "I know how to mind my manners."

"When you feel like it," Jude whispered back.

"Boys, be nice." Aunt Maggie frowned at them.

Magistrate Witherspoon gestured to the head of the table. "I apologize in advance; you'll all have to sit on the ground. But we spread out our biggest quilts so you won't get dirty."

"Thank you so much, this all looks wonderful." Aunt Maggie sat down, and the children followed suit, being careful not to squash the tiny dogs that bounded around their heels, or the errant children that ran up, touched their shoes, and ran back to their friends as though it were some kind of dare.

The entire town sat around the rest of the table, and soon everyone was passing out food and eating.

Though the food was much smaller than the children were used to, it tasted better than dishes served at the finest castle feasts. Tiny biscuits dripped with golden honey, and teensy fried eggs that must have come from miniature chickens had just the right amount of salt and pepper. There was roast beef and loaves of bread and best of all, dozens of miniature pies with perfect, flaky crusts. As soon as one of the children emptied a plate, an Eep person refilled it.

Before long, Celeste had become used to the strange little people, and no longer started when one of them rose up from a seat on their long legs.

It took some time, but the children finally had their fill. They leaned away from the table, relaxing in the springy, soft grass.

Magistrate Witherspoon glanced around the table. "Now that we've shared our lunch, we must tell you why we asked you to come." He sighed, a long, gusty sigh for such a small person, and rubbed the bushy beard that spilled down over the front of his suit. "It pains me to speak the words, but soon my people will be marching off to war."

The biscuit Celeste had just swallowed turned into a painful lump on its way down her throat.

"Oh!" Aunt Maggie pressed her palm against her heart. "That *is* terrible and unexpected news! What caused this to happen? I thought Rellyland had been a place of peace for the last five hundred years."

"Five hundred and three," said Mrs. Witherspoon. "But that doesn't matter now." She hugged Lemon, who was sitting next to her. "I worry the most about our children. What will they do while we're off fighting?"

The magistrate patted her hand. "We'll figure something out. Duchess Margarite always has wonderful ideas. We'll most surely win, now that she and the royal children are here."

Aunt Maggie examined a tiny baked potato on the end of a fork the size of a safety pin. "Of course we'll help if we can. But war?" She shook her head. "I never thought I'd live to see the day when war would come to Rellyland. Can you please explain how this came about?"

"It involves the Opes," the magistrate said. An anger crept into his voice, and his bushy eyebrows met in a point over his nose.

At these words, the Eeps began to bang their spoons on the table. Some of them booed and hissed

"The Opes?" Aunt Maggie raised her eyebrows. "I thought you just ignored each other."

"We did," said a man with an especially large bowtie. "But it's come to a point where we cannot ignore them any longer. It used to be they'd whisper rude things when we met by chance in the woods, but now it's become worse."

"They've built a catapult," said a woman wearing a blue hat with yellow streamers. "And they use it to fling rocks with mean notes tied to them into our village. They've destroyed two barns and a watermelon crop."

From what Celeste had heard of war, it was a horrible thing. *Why would you go to war over a few mean words?*

"Don't you say unkind things as well?" said Aunt Maggie. She pointed to a long seesaw-looking object in the field past the village. "And isn't that a catapult over there?"

"They started it!" Magistrate Witherspoon leapt to his feet, his moustache quivering. "They are putting our lives in danger and we simply cannot tolerate it anymore! We must fight them."

"Well I'm sure if you could just get together and talk it over . . ." Aunt Maggie began.

The magistrate pounded the table with a tiny fist. "We cannot and we will not. We will go to war."

"Oh dear." Aunt Maggie clasped her hands in front of her. "I had no idea you people were so bloodthirsty."

"We aren't, usually," insisted Mrs. Witherspoon. "But when one is driven, one must act."

Aunt Maggie put her face in her hands. "Dare I ask, dear Eeps . . . what do you want me to do? Why did you ask me for help?"

The Magistrate's sullen face brightened. "Well, er . . . you possess a size and strength none of us can claim. We thought you could . . . lead the charge? The war would be over before it started. And you might not even have to stomp anyone."

Aunt Maggie blinked. "*Stomp* anyone?"

The man with the large bowtie nodded. "Those Opes would probably flee in terror! Especially if the royal children come as well."

Aunt Maggie stood and wiped the last of the pie crumbs from her lips. "People of Eep, I am sorry about your problem. I love you and care for you all dearly, as though you were my own family. But I refuse to assist in any sort of war where anyone could be hurt or any life could be lost. If you would like me to lead in some kind of peace talk, I would be more than happy to help. We will stay for one more night to give you time to think it over."

The magistrate folded his arms. "We are very displeased by this decision. Everyone here agrees that there will be no peace talks. We have waited for the Opes apology long enough. It is time for action."

All the villagers nodded solemnly.

Mrs. Witherspoon spread out her hands. "We are at your mercy, Duchess Margarite. If you choose not to help us there's not much we can do. But please, think of the children."

Aunt Maggie's cheeks reddened. "And what of the Ope children?" she demanded. "Their lives are just as precious. I refuse to help anyone with a war, and that's final."

Celeste breathed a sigh of relief. She certainly didn't want to get involved in a war.

Lemon tugged at Celeste's sleeve. "Do you want to come and play with us?" she asked, her big blue eyes hopeful.

Celeste glanced up at Aunt Maggie. "May we?"

Aunt Maggie waved her hands. "Yes, I'm going to stay and try to talk some sense into these good people. You three go for a bit."

The Eep children led Celeste, Jude and Torrin back to the village.

"Wait here while we get our game things," said Huxley.

Huxley strode over to one of the tallest poles. He gathered his long legs beneath him, almost like a frog, and sprung into the air. Up and up he soared, until he grabbed the lip of the wide base that topped the pole. He scrambled up and went inside the little house.

"I wish I could jump like that," said Celeste. *Even if it meant looking a bit strange.* She imagined herself scampering along the outside towers and turrets of the palace. *Sir Gringle and Lady Gertle would never catch me then.*

"Your legs would probably get all tangled up if you didn't know how to manage them," said Jude.

"True," said Celeste. "I guess I should be happy with the way I am." Nevertheless, it was highly entertaining to watch.

The Eep children spent all afternoon teaching the three royal children how to play a game they called Nobscottle, which was a mix between Red Rover and dodge ball. There was plenty of running and jumping with just a slight sense of danger. Though the Eeps were smaller than the royals, their long legs made them worthy opponents.

Jude received a bruise on his knee which he was quite proud of. Torrin bashed his head against a tree and felt it might turn into a proper black eye later on, if he was lucky.

Right when Celeste had obtained the noggin ball and was rounding the fifth base to the home mark, Aunt Maggie came to the edge of the field.

"Children, we must go. These people already fed us a week's worth of food for lunch. Let's not put them out for supper."

"Are we still having a war?" Lemon asked her.

"Of course we are," said Huxley before Aunt Maggie could reply. He kicked a tiny pebble across the ground. "Sometimes adults can be so stubborn."

Aunt Maggie's shoulders slumped. "Eep children, I'm sorry."

A determined glint came into Huxley's eye, and he squared his small shoulders. "That's all right. You did your best."

"Come children. Maybe we'll come back after the war, if there's anyone left," Aunt Maggie added, glaring at the magistrate and his wife.

Magistrate Witherspoon stared down at his feet and said nothing.

Celeste stumbled back to camp with a heavy heart. They'd had such fun with their new friends. At the palace, they were never allowed to play with village urchins or the children of the servants. The only times they'd seen other young people were on rare occasions when travelling dignitaries brought their children, and those youngsters were also only allowed to play croquet or chess, or sometimes have fencing matches with their fake swords.

"Shame Lester missed everything. He loves coming here," said Aunt Maggie over her shoulder.

Lester still hung from his place on Maggie's back where he'd been for most of the day. His furry little eyes were shut tight.

Aunt Maggie found the Windlesoar, much to Celeste's relief, and uncovered it quickly.

Everyone worked together to remove the tarp and set up their campsite, which was as nice as it had been the night before.

They sat around a crackling fire, eating bread and cheese.

"Aunt Maggie, Mama and Papa aren't wondering where we are, are they?" asked Celeste.

"Heavens, child you're just now asking that?" Aunt Maggie shook her head.

"Children can be such selfish creatures," said Lester who'd awoken half an hour before. He crunched a cookie thoughtfully between his sharp teeth.

"Are they worried about us?" asked Jude. "You think Papa will send search parties throughout the land?"

"Nothing that dramatic is going to happen," said Aunt Maggie. "I sent Lester with a note to your parents explaining we would be gone for a few days."

At least we won't get into trouble when we get home, Celeste thought. But she wondered what would happen to the Eeps after they went to war.

9

Meeting the Opes

A tiny hand patted Celeste's shoulder. She opened her eyes sleepily and peered around the tent. Everything was dark. Crickets chirped outside, along with a chorus of other animal sounds she couldn't identify. Aunt Maggie snored softly on the cot beside her.

A small white face stared into hers.

Lemon.

The Eep girl put a finger to her lips and beckoned for Celeste to follow her outside.

Jude and Torrin were already standing by the blackened fire, rubbing their eyes, and blinking sleepily. Several Eep children were gathered around them.

"We're sorry to bother you," said Huxley, who stood beside Torrin. "But we need your help."

Lemon moved toward the little footbridge that crossed the stream. "Come over here where we can talk. We don't want to wake the Duchess." She glanced up at the sky. "And I'm sure Lester isn't far."

"Shouldn't we tell Aunt Maggie?" Jude asked. "Won't we need her help too?"

"She's an adult." Lemon wrinkled her nose. "You're children like us, even though you're big. The duchess would scare our friends."

"What friends?" asked Torrin.

"Come with us, and you'll see."

The Eep children led them in the opposite direction of the village, through the dense woods.

Colorful lights from glowmies filled the air with flashes of pink, gold, and lavender.

The Eep children raised their hands in the air. "Come, glowmies! Come to us and light our way!"

The glowmies flew in closer, until the path was almost bright as day.

Celeste wished a glowmie would rest on her finger so she could study it better, they were such pretty little things. But they simply fluttered around her, some so close they brushed her cheek with their soft, silken wings.

The group left the tree line and walked along the edge of a wide bluff. A moonlit valley fanned out below them, dotted with dozens of small mounds, looking like ocean waves on the land. A mountain towered in the distance.

"What is this place?" asked Jude.

"Shhh," Huxley hissed. "The people of Ope have very good hearing."

"The people of Ope!" Torrin yelped. "You mean the ones who started the war?"

"Please don't be so loud." Lemon put a finger to her lips and began to creep down the slope to the right of the hills.

Everyone followed her, until they came upon the bank of the river again, where it sprung out from between the mounds.

A circle of glowmies had settled down on some rocks. Huddled within the light was another crowd of tiny children. Except these young ones didn't have long legs like the Eeps. They talked and waved their hands, which were larger than most peoples and ended with long, spindly fingers.

"These are the Ope children," whispered Huxley. "They use their hands to dig underground. The Opes have amazing underground cities. I wish I could see them."

The Ope children rose to their feet as the group approached.

All of them were dressed in pajamas, and they all wore scowls, frowns, or pouts on their faces.

One of them, a little girl in a pink fluffy nightgown, held out her long-fingered hand. "Royal children, we're thankful you've come. We hope you'll help us in our time of need."

"But how can we help you?" said Jude. "We're only children ourselves."

"Yes, but you're big children," said Lemon with a hopeful smile, her face shining in the light of the glowmies. "A wise and great person lives near here. He used to help our peoples in times of hardship, but now he won't talk to us anymore. He lives up on a tall mountain. None of us can climb that high. But you could. His name is the Great EepOpe."

"When would we go?" asked Celeste. "Aunt Maggie said we're leaving first thing tomorrow morning."

Huxley rubbed his chin. "You have to go tonight, right away." He got on his knees and clasped his hands before him. "Please help us out! We're friends with the Ope children. We want to be able to play with each other without having to keep it a secret."

An Ope boy added, "We'd like to visit each other's homes and play Nobscottle together. Right now, whenever an Eep sees an Ope, or an Ope sees an Eep, they start shouting mean things and throwing sticks, or dirt clods. Sometimes even fruits and vegetables."

Lemon twisted a strand of golden hair around her finger. "We don't like that. And we certainly don't want to get hurt in a war."

"Or see our mommies and daddies get hurt," said a very little Ope boy with curly hair.

Jude held up his hand. "Give us a moment." He pulled Celeste and Torrin aside to a cluster of trees where the Eep and Ope children couldn't hear their conversation.

"What do you think we should do?" he whispered. "We should be in agreement about this."

"I don't know." Torrin scratched his head. "What if we get hurt? What if Aunt Maggie leaves without us?"

Celeste bit her lip. "I hadn't even thought of that. That would be awful."

Jude frowned. "I doubt Aunt Maggie would ever leave us behind. Especially if we sent the Eep children back to camp to leave a note telling her where we went. Sounds like we'd return before morning anyway. I think we must at least try. If our kingdom were going to war, we'd want someone to help."

Torrin hung his head. "I hadn't thought of it that way."

"Yes," Celeste nodded. "I think we should do it."

When Jude announced the decision, the Ope children clapped their broad hands, and the Eep children danced a jig on their long legs.

They crept down into the valley past the hills that covered up the Opes' homes. The Eep and Ope children tiptoed ahead in a long, single-file line.

Celeste thought about all the Ope mamas and papas sleeping down in the underground cities. She wondered if they had cats, dogs, chickens, horses, and cows like the Eeps. She didn't see anything moving about. *Perhaps they bring them out to graze during the day and lock them up at night.*

At last, the group made it past all the little hills, across the wide field, and to the foot of the mountain.

"I can see why you needed us," said Torrin, squinting up at the narrow trail. "But if you can't climb the mountain, how do you know the Great EepOpe is still living up there?"

"We know," said a little girl, "because we see the smoke drifting through the sky from his chimney. Every now and then we hear him crashing through the forest to gather food. We never disturb him."

"But we haven't heard or seen him in a long time," said a little Ope boy. "He's awfully grouchy. And big. We're far too scared to talk to him ourselves."

"You'd better get going. But be careful," said Lemon. "Don't let the giant growlies get you."

"Growlies?" Torrin yelled. "Wait a minute . . . What's a growlie?"

But the children had all vanished into the thick grass like grasshoppers.

"Great." Torrin folded his arms. "I'm not going up there to be eaten."

"Come on," said Jude. "We've come all this way. Do you really want to leave all those children to deal with a war?"

"Yes, Torrin, we have to go." Celeste set her foot on the beginning of the path. "It doesn't look too steep. We can do this."

"We're going with or without you," said Jude.

"You mean you'd leave me down here?" Torrin's mouth dropped open. "What about not deserting your own flesh and blood and all that talk?"

Jude clapped a hand on his brother's shoulder. "Papa also taught us not to shirk our responsibility. No matter what lies ahead, it's better faced together."

"Oh, all right." Torrin trudged after them, moving as though his feet were tied down with leaden weights.

The children walked the winding mountain path with minimal stumbling, thanks to the light of the friendly glowmies, which hovered all around them.

As they neared the top, Celeste elbowed Torrin. "Hey, does it look like the glowmies are changing color?"

"I see that," said Torrin "It seems like–are they turning red?"

And it was true. Cheerful golds, pinks and blues deepened into dark scarlet.

"Maybe they're hungry? Or sick?" Jude suggested.

"Or maybe they're trying to warn us. I knew we shouldn't have come up here." Torrin stopped.

Celeste suddenly froze in place,   as though her feet had been rooted to the ground. "Did you hear that?"

10

The Great EepOpe

Brush and trees created a wide fringe at the mountain's top. Through this thicket came an awful growling noise.

Once at the castle, when Celeste had been only four years old, a man had brought in a trained bear that could do tricks. The bear was friendly, but he'd been trained to growl in a frightening way.

Sometimes, the younger dogs in the stables would growl and play with each other, pretending to be fearsome.

None of the growls she'd ever heard sounded like this. The sound sent chills down her spine and made the hairs on the back of her neck stand up.

Jude squared his shoulders and pushed through the trees.

Torrin groaned. "Why does he always have to be so brave and noble?" But he followed him.

"Don't leave me here all by myself!" wailed Celeste. She went after her brothers, every step on shaky knees.

When she pushed through the trees, she saw the glowmies clumped together, hovering in the air. Jude stood in the middle of a clearing, stock-still, with Torrin right behind him.

The most terrifying creature Celeste had ever seen rose up before her brothers. Even in her papa's books about beasts, dragons, and werewolves, she'd never seen a monster this scary. It was bigger than the tallest soldier in her father's army. A shaggy coat of fur covered its body, curling down to the ground, full of twigs and leaves and other messy things. Glittery red eyes glared at her brothers, and teeth long as her hand stuck out of its mouth in uneven spikes. The creature opened this giant mouth and let out a bellow while it pawed the ground with enormous clawed feet.

Jude darted to the left while Torrin took off to the right. But Celeste couldn't move as the beast charged her.

"Celeste! Look out!" Torrin shouted. In a sudden blur her brother swept in the way, a giant stick in his hand. He whacked the beast on the nose.

The monster roared again and chased after Torrin, who darted in and out of the trees.

My brother really does care about me. Celeste's heart pounded in her ears. *It's nice to still be alive.* And then– "Look out!" she shouted. "Jude, do something!"

The beast was only a few paces from Torrin now.

Jude jumped up and down, waving his hands in the air. "What should I do? I don't know what to do!"

"You always know what to do!" Celeste screamed.

Torrin zigzagged through the brush and rocks, the monster lumbering after. Finally, he shinnied up a tree. "Go away, you mean old thing!" he shouted from the branches.

The beast grabbed the trunk of the tree and begin to shake it. Torrin was tossed around like a rag doll. He shut his eyes, gripping a thick branch with both arms.

Suddenly, a black leathery shape flew out of the sky, darting into the monster's face. The creature flapped its wide wings over the monster's eyes. The growlie roared and let go of the tree trunk, pawing at the flying beast.

"Oh it's Lester!" shouted Celeste. "Be careful, Lester! Don't let it get you!"

"What in all of Rellyland is going on out here!" boomed a voice from the stand of rocks. "Snarfle, what's happening? You're supposed to fetch me if there's a disturbance."

A man came out of the rocks. He was taller than the Eeps or the Opes but still much shorter than the children. His legs were long and lean, and his rather large hands ended with long, spindly fingers. He was dressed in a worn, brown robe with a hood. A thin beard dangled from his chin.

The Monster ran to the man's side, panting like a dog. It rubbed its giant head against his shoulder.

Celeste's eyes widened. Could that really be the same beast?

Torrin climbed down the tree and came over to Celeste. His breath came in gasps and his lips trembled.

A dark scowl covered his face. "Does that creature belong to you?" he asked the man.

"Why, yes." The old man picked a twig from the growlie's fur. "It wouldn't be safe to live up here without some sort of protection. All sorts of vicious creatures live in these woods. Speaking of which," he said, giving them a very hard stare. "Who are you and why are you disturbing my peace at such a late hour?"

Lester flapped down from the top of the tree where he had settled after the fight. "Pardon these children, Mr. EepOpe," he said. "I am responsible for them. Though I can't begin to tell you why they're here." He raised his batty eyebrow at the children. "Perhaps one of you can explain?"

The children all began to talk at once, each screaming their side of the story. Torrin's face was very red, and Celeste felt like plunking down in the dirt and having a good cry.

The EepOpe held up his hands. "Children, why don't you come inside my home and we'll have a bit of early breakfast. You can tell me everything in a civilized manner." He glared at each one in turn. "Or we can stay out here and scream our heads off. Either way is fine with me."

Jude glanced over at Lester.

Lester shrugged his bat shoulders. "Don't look at me. You children decided to go off on your own. I'm only here to fly in the faces of monsters for you." He paused. "But Mr. EepOpe is absolutely safe."

"Of course I'm safe," the Great EepOpe scoffed. "Even Snarfle is harmless. He's all roar and no bite." He turned and shuffled in the direction of the hills, with the growlie bounding along beside him.

They approached a cavern with a purple, triangle-shaped door. The Great EepOpe pulled on a curious, spoon-shaped, silver lever and the door swung open.

"Come on in, children. Let's discuss this like the reasonable people we are. Or should be, anyway."

The room was cozy and warm, and a cheery fire crackled from a hearth in the rock wall.

Celeste wondered where the smoke was let out, and pictured the lazy threads floating in the sky somewhere above the mountain.

The Great EepOpe gestured to a pile of knobby cushions in one corner. "Take a pillow and find a spot."

Jude picked a royal blue cushion, Torrin chose a red one, and Celeste pulled out an orange pillow with purple fringe.

The children arranged the pillows on the floor in a circle around the Great EepOpe.

The EepOpe went over to a round, wooden table and came back carrying a platter. The wonderful scent of chocolate chip cookies wafted through the air.

"No sense being hungry while we talk." The Great EepOpe passed the cookies to each of the royal children.

"I'll take one of those, thank you," said Lester, grabbing a cookie. He flapped up to a lamp that hung from a pole and stuffed the snack into his mouth. His cheeks filled out like a chipmunk's.

A few crumbs dropped down on Torrin's head. "Hey!" he protested.

The Great EepOpe sat on a stool topped by one of the knobby cushions, towering over the children. He pulled back his hood, and a great tuft of white hair sprang up, almost brushing the roof of the cavern.

"Now that we're settled," he said, clasping his long fingers beneath his chin. "What brings three–royal, by the looks of you–children all the way to Rellyland to visit my mountain in the dead of night? Surely you didn't come to see the view."

Jude brushed crumbs off his lap. "No, Sir. We came by the request of the Eep and Ope children. Their parents are preparing for a terrible war and the children have asked us to beg for your wisdom. How can they stop the war, oh Great EepOpe?"

Pride welled up in Celeste's soul. Jude could sound so eloquent and princely when he chose to. *Of course, it would probably be better if his face weren't smeared with chocolate.*

The Great EepOpe frowned, and wrinkles flowed down his forehead to his eyebrows. "A war, huh? I wondered when it would come to that. Surprised it hasn't already."

"Can you do something to help them?" asked Celeste.

The Great EepOpe gave a long sigh, and the long hairs of his mustache blew out into the air like dandelion seeds, then settled back down.

"No," he finally said.

Torrin jumped up from his cushion. "Why not? The Eeps and Opes are your neighbors. Why can't you help them?"

"Tell me something, children. Duchess Margarite's bat friend has come with you. Which means the Duchess must be close by. She probably brought you here in one of her contraptions. Am I correct?"

Torrin nodded. His hands were clenched into fists, his knuckles turning white.

"So." The Great EepOpe shifted on his stool. "I'm willing to wager another tray of cookies that she already tried to speak reason to one of the Magistrates of the great towns of Eep and Ope. Or perhaps both?"

Jude hung his head. "Yes sir, she did."

"I see," said the Great EepOpe. "And would I also be correct to assume that they would not listen to her?"

"No, they wouldn't." Torrin sank back down to the floor. "But that's why the children asked us to come up–"

The Great EepOpe held up his hand. "Say no more." His bushy eyebrows knitted together. "No, children, I'm sorry. Nothing I can do will help people who won't listen to reason. Tell the Eep and Ope children to go to the great green stone in the middle of the forest, far away from the villages and war. After the battle I'll try to help them in any way that I can. I'll bring them food and blankets and mend the injured folks, if possible. But I cannot stop this war."

He jumped off his perch and pointed to the cavern entrance. "Dawn is about to break. Go find your aunt and get away before the battle commences. The Eeps' and Opes' weapons may be small, but they could still harm you."

The children rose from their cushions, and under the Great EepOpe's watchful glare, stacked the pillows back in the corner. Celeste followed behind her brothers, all three with their heads hanging down.

The first light of dawn streaked the sky with beautiful pinks and blues, but it didn't cheer up Celeste. All she could think about was the terrible war that would happen soon to the tiny people below.

Tears dribbled down her cheeks and she tried to swallow the lump forming in her throat.

Suddenly a thought struck her. *I'm a royal princess.* Throwing back her shoulders, she stuck out her chin and marched into the cave.

The Great EepOpe was snatching another cookie from the platter. He raised his eyebrows when he saw her. "Little girl, did you forget something?"

"Yes," said Celeste, in the haughtiest, most princessy tone she could muster. "I forgot I'm a royal. If I wished, I could order you to try and stop the war." She took a deep breath. "But I'm not going to do that, because Mama says royals shouldn't be bullies. So I'm going to ask you nicely. Please, Great EepOpe. Please try and stop the war."

The Great EepOpe stared at her for a long moment, a cookie poised in front of his mouth. He gave a dry chuckle. "You were going to order me, eh? Don't forget, little girl, you're not in your kingdom anymore. I don't have to obey your commands."

The brave thoughts that had built up inside Celeste came out in a whoosh, and she bowed her head, blinking hard to keep more tears from flowing.

The Great EepOpe patted her shoulder. "But you did say please, and you're right. I should try one more time."

He went outside, and Celeste followed.

Jude and Torrin waited at the edge of the forest, a healthy distance from the growlie, who was now sleeping in a giant heap of fur.

"Why did you go back in there? What's going on?" asked Torrin.

The Great EepOpe waved to Lester, who hung upside-down from a branch of the very tree Torrin had climbed to get away from the growlie. "My bat friend, would you please come down? I have a plan to help the villagers and I'll need you to fly to your mistress to tell her about it."

He stroked his beard. "Children, I won't be coming with you, because the Eeps and Opes will run away if they see me. They've convinced themselves I'm not right in the head and they won't listen. But a disaster is waiting to befall both of the villages. A few elken-elves told me about it yesterday and Snarfles and I were going down to try to fix it. However, I think it could serve a better purpose." He rubbed his hands together. "Here's what you need to do."

11

Making Repairs

Celeste and Torrin crashed through the forest as fast as their legs would carry them. Blue-and-yellow striped birds flew in startled bursts from the bushes.

"Oh, I hope we make it before the war starts!" Celeste gasped. Her legs ached and she longed to stop and catch her breath.

"I hope the Opes listen to Jude," said Torrin.

The Eep children followed them, keeping pace with their frog-like hops.

Aunt Maggie waited for them a short distance from the Eeps village. For the first time since they'd met her, she looked anxious. "Children." She enfolded them in her arms. "I was so worried. Lester told me to meet you here, and I hope you have a good reason for running off like that. Where is your brother?"

"He's with the Opes," replied Torrin.

"The Opes?" Aunt Maggie frowned. "Is he in danger?"

Celeste gulped. "I hope not. We promise we'll explain everything, Aunt Maggie, but right now we have to rush to the Eeps' village and stop the war!"

"How are you going to do that?" asked Aunt Maggie.

"No time to explain." Torrin looked over his shoulder towards the village.

Aunt Maggie dropped her hands to her sides. "Very well. I guess there's nothing to lose. Be careful, children."

Celeste dashed off again, with Torrin right behind.

The Eep children hopped around their feet. "Hurry, hurry," they cried. "Hurry, hurry, hurry!"

Celeste reached the pole houses. "Eeps? She called out. Magistrate Witherspoon?"

No one answered. The children darted in and out of barns and sheds, but came out, shaking their heads. Tiny dogs barked at them from pens and a few cows chewed miniscule cuds in fenced-off pastures.

Torrin tipped his head to the side. "Is that music?"

"I think so," said Celeste.

They followed the thin melody to the open plain past the village, where they'd eaten their lunch the day before.

The adult Eeps were fanned out across the field in lines of ten, marching beside a catapult and several tiny cannons. Horses and oxen had been hitched to carts, straining to pull the heavy loads. The colorful clothing had been exchanged for drab, mud-colored uniforms. Each person carried a weapon of some sort, a spear, a bow, or daggers the size of toothpicks, except for a group of four Eeps who were playing instruments. The melody they played was bright and cheerful, in contrast to the fierce frowns they all wore on their faces.

"Forward!" shouted Magistrate Witherspoon from the back of a miniature purple pony. He waved a gleaming curved sword. "We'll teach those Opes to call us names!"

"Wait!" shouted Celeste. She ran in front of the catapult. "You all have to stop! A great danger is threatening your village!"

"We know." Mrs. Witherspoon was perched on the seat of a wagon by her husband's horse. "That's why we're going to war. I thought we explained that already."

"No," said Torrin. "You don't understand. It's even a worse danger than that. You have to come to the riverbank. The dam . . . it's going to burst!"

"What?" the Magistrate's eyes bulged. "How can that be?"

"It's true, Papa," said Lemon. "We saw it. Water is leaking all over. The thing could fail at any moment."

The magistrate sheathed his sword. "What of it? Our homes are on tall poles. The water won't bother us. The Opes, however . . ." he rubbed his hands, and a crafty smile spread over his face.

"But, Father," said Huxley. "You don't understand. If the bank completely bursts, the wall of water will be high enough to flood our homes. Not only that but it will wipe out our crops and our animals. We have to do something!"

The other villagers began murmuring to each other. Their faces were very white.

Celeste held her breath. Would the villagers listen? Would their plan work?

Aunt Maggie swept over the field, looking every bit the duchess she was, even in her old, battered hat and worn travelling clothes. "Magistrate Witherspoon, I think it's best we listen to the children. You can always have your war tomorrow; it's not going anywhere. But you could lose everything if you don't take action now."

The Magistrate sighed and took off his tin-pail helmet, dropping it on the ground beside him. "Argh! I suppose we better go see what's going on." He grabbed his fancy top hat from the wagon where his wife was sitting and placed it on his head.

The Eeps led the way through the forest, followed by Torrin, Celeste and Aunt Maggie, until they reached the dam, which was only a few minutes away.

Celeste figured it was about the same distance as the Opes' village. *If we were in the Windlesoar, it would look like a giant "V," with the dam at the bottom point and the two villages on the top points.*

Jude and the Ope people were all waiting for them at the riverbank.

In the daylight, Celeste was surprised to see that the Opes were just as clean and shiny as the Eeps, without a speck of dirt on their faces, despite their underground style of living. And like the Eeps, they were also dressed in battle clothes and makeshift armor.

Jude rushed over to hug Celeste and Torrin. "Huzzah! You convinced them to come!" He stepped back, his cheeks flaming. "I mean, um, good job, both of you."

The Eeps and Opes stood in two groups, several yards apart. They glared at each other, muttering amongst themselves.

"Oh dear," Lemon hooked her arm around Celeste's thumb. "I hope this works."

Celeste gave her friend a gentle hug. "It will. It has to!"

"What are you people doing here?" Magistrate Witherspoon shouted at an Ope villager who was wearing a special top hat, similar to his own.

"That's the Ope Magistrate," Aunt Maggie whispered to the children.

"This giant boy, who calls himself a prince came with our children while we were preparing for war." The

Ope Magistrate pointed to Jude. "He told us to come check the dam, and he was right, Look! it could burst at any moment!"

"Our homes will all be destroyed!" wailed another Ope man, who carried a shield that looked as though it might have once been the door of an oven.

The dam rose before them, a giant clay bank three times as tall as Aunt Maggie's head. Logs and stumps had been piled beside it, along with a jumble of rocks, boulders, and other natural materials. Throughout the wall were several holes where water trickled through in tiny streams, but in a few places it gushed in mini floods. The ground around the bank was muddy and in some places ankle-deep in water–at least for the royal children. For the Eeps and the Opes, the water would reach the waists of even the tallest among them.

"Eeps and Opes, this is what happens when you fail to work together," said Aunt Maggie. "For centuries you have kept this dam operational. But now it's falling apart. Why haven't you watched and repaired the holes as they happened?"

The two magistrates pointed to each other and said, at the same time, "It's his fault."

Aunt Maggie sighed.

"At least the big people are here, right?" said an Ope woman. "Maybe they can fix it?"

"Too many holes," said the Ope magistrate. "They can't do it fast enough. The thing could crumble at any time."

"Of course, we will help you as much as we can," said Aunt Maggie. "But some places are too high for even us to reach."

"Oh what will we do?" Mrs. Witherspoon wrung her hands. "Perhaps we should run back to our villages and save what we can."

"No need to do that," said Celeste. "We have an idea but . . . you'll have to work together."

"Work with those dirty ground dwellers!" scoffed Magistrate Witherspoon. "Surely not!"

The magistrate of the Opes folded his arms and frowned. "You airheads will mess up everything, anyway."

While they were glaring at each other, a large chunk of dirt fell from the side of the embankment and a stream of water shot out from the resulting hole. It knocked both of the magistrates flat on their backs. They both jumped up, wet and sputtering, their splendid hats floating away.

"Please, Daddy." Lemon clasped her hands in front of her. "Please work together!"

"All right, all right!" shouted Magistrate Witherspoon, clutching the wet mop of hair on the top of his head. "What do we need to do?"

Jude pointed to a gigantic mud puddle that was forming on the edge of the pool. "The Opes can scoop up clay here and make mud clods."

Celeste nodded. "And you Eeps can leap up to the top of the dam, where even us big people can't reach, and patch up the holes."

Torrin added, "the big people will gather more rocks and logs to pile in front of the dam so it won't have problems again."

The Magistrates looked at each other with wide eyes.

"It might just work," said Magistrate Witherspoon.

"You know it's a splendid idea," said Aunt Maggie in an exasperated tone. She picked up a large rock by the side of the bank. "Now let's get started."

Everyone helped. The Opes, from youngest to oldest, scooped-out mud and packed it together to make goopy balls of muck. An Eep jumped to the top of a stump and pointed out places that needed to be patched, while all the other Eeps leapt to pack mud in the spots. The three Royal children and their aunt moved large logs and rocks to the base of the dam.

Celeste's hands ached from the constant lugging and stacking. She stepped back and surveyed the bank. *No more streams of water.* She smiled. "I think it's working!" she said to Torrin.

"I guess the Great EepOpe knew what he was talking about." Torrin wiped his forehead, smearing mud all over his face.

At lunch time, several Eep and Ope people brought baskets of food in wagons. Everyone washed up in the lake as best they could.

The magistrates agreed the crisis was over for now, though they would have to continue to work on the bank for many months to make sure leaks didn't happen again.

Celeste looked around as she munched on her sandwich. Though people had washed their hands and faces for the meal, the river clay wasn't easy to remove. Everyone's clothes and hair were still matted with mud. With all the muck it was hard to tell who were Eeps and who were Opes.

The tiny people looked tired but happy, and both the Eeps and Opes joked with each other as they ate their lunch. Not mean jokes to make fun of each other, but stories everyone seemed to enjoy.

Celeste smiled. "I think the war is over," she whispered to Torrin.

"I think so too." Torrin smiled. "And we helped."

"Yeah, we did." Jude popped the tiniest cupcake imaginable into his mouth and chewed thoughtfully. He picked up another one. "This must be how Mama and Papa feel when they help people. They have really important jobs. Someday, we'll be doing this every day."

"Not me," said Torrin. "I'm the younger son. I don't have to be king. I get to stay a Prince and do fun things." He munched a sausage thoughtfully. "I suppose I could help people sometimes. Maybe during the holidays." Aunt Maggie approached their picnic spot, Lester folded up on her back in his usual place. "Children, I'm pretty tired out, and from what I understand, you were up most of the night."

"Yeah," Jude hung his head. "We're sorry, Aunt Maggie. We should've told you where we were going."

"Yes, you should have." Aunt Maggie frowned. "I need to be able to trust the three of you. And know you trust me when you need help." She ruffled Jude's hair. "Especially since I might want you to come with me on another adventure."

The children gazed at each other with shining eyes.

The journey to Rellyland had been wonderful, but Celeste hadn't considered they might be allowed to go on another just like it.

"For now, shall we go to the campsite and take a nap?" said Aunt Maggie.

"Finally," came Lester's sleepy voice from Aunt Maggie's back. "Humans want to sleep during the day like normal folks."

Aunt Maggie nodded. "After the nap, you three can clean up camp before we fly home to repay me for running off last night."

"Sounds fair," said Torrin. "But I don't need a nap. I'm not at all sleepy." He yawned.

Aunt Maggie raised her eyebrows and smiled. "Not a bit, huh? Maybe you can tidy the entire camp by yourself while the rest of us get a nap. What do you think, children?" she nodded to Jude and Celeste.

"Fine with me." Celeste shrugged.

"No fair!" Torrin folded his arms.

"I'm just teasing," said Aunt Maggie. "You'll all work together."

A short time later, the Eep and Ope people followed the little travelling party to the footbridge. They'd cleaned themselves and were dressed in their brightly colored outfits again.

Magistrate Witherspoon shook hands all around by grasping everyone's pinky fingers and jumping up and down.

Mrs. Witherspoon handed them each one last cupcake. "Thank you so much for helping to save our village."

"Don't forget about the Great EepOpe," said Jude. "If he hadn't told us about the dam we'd have never known."

The Eep and Ope children gathered around, hugging the children's ankles.

"Come back and play with us soon." Lemon's cheeks shone with tiny tears as she came up to Celeste. "Thank you for helping us get our friends back and keep everyone safe." Her green eyes were wide under the brim of her floppy-brimmed hat. "You're my best friend of all."

"Oh!" a tear dripped off the end of Celeste's nose and splattered to the ground, narrowly missing the Eep girl. "I'll miss you too. Maybe we can come back soon."

12

Home Again

The next day the Windlesoar returned to the roof of the castle.

Celeste sat still in the basket after they'd landed, sleepy and filled with wonder by all the things she'd seen. Sometimes she still pinched herself to make sure it hadn't all been a dream.

Torrin rested his chin in his hands, light from spaces in the basket-weave playing on his face. "I guess it's back to chess and croquet again."

"Maybe not," said Celeste. "Didn't you hear Aunt Maggie say we might get to go again? So even if we have boring days here, we might have more adventures to look forward to soon."

"I hope so." Torrin sighed.

"Children, come on out," Aunt Maggie called.

Celeste helped empty out the baskets and cover the Windlesoar with a tarp–not the invisibility one but a regular canvas one this time. She gathered her belongings and followed Aunt Maggie to the tower room where she lived.

After everything was settled, Aunt Maggie led them to the door. "Children, I've had such fun. You are the best travelling companions anyone could wish for."

Lester, who was hanging from a candelabra, made a noise in his throat.

"Well, except for Lester, of course." Aunt Maggie rolled her eyes. "You should go down and see your parents to let them know you've returned. But please come and see me again soon."

"Of course we will." Jude shook her hand.

The three royal children trooped down the secret staircase.

It was strange to be home again, in the enclosed stone walls. Celeste missed the fresh air, trees, and flowers of

Rellyland. *But I missed home too. Oh, I hope we can go back soon!*

The King and Queen were in the throne room, looking through papers.

When the Queen caught sight of them, she jumped up from her throne, scattering papers through the air like flat, white butterflies. She ran to the children and enveloped them in her arms all at once. "Darlings, I've missed you so. Did you have a wonderful time with your aunt?"

"It was amazing," said Jude. "Thank you for letting us go."

The king stepped down beside his wife and gave each of them his own, slightly more dignified, hugs. "Didn't get into too much trouble, did you?"

"Torrin got chased by a growlie," said Celeste.

"Tattle-tale." Torrin frowned.

"I only told because he did it to protect me." Celeste folded her arms. "He was a hero."

Torrin covered his mouth with his hand, but not in time to hide his smile.

"Aw, a growlie's growl is worse than his bite," said the Queen.

Jude's jaw dropped. "But if you know what a growlie is, then that means . . ."

"Oh yes, we've been to Rellyland," said his mother. "And lots more places. Before all of you came along, we went with Aunt Maggie."

"And we're so glad she's willing to take you," finished the King.

The doors to the throne room burst open, and in rushed Lady Gertle and Sir Gringle. "There they are!" Lady Gertle sat on a stool and fanned herself with her strange hat. "Oh your majesties, we've been looking for these naughty children for days."

Sir Gringle's jowls were red, and his eyebrows knitted over his beak-like nose. "Yes. Look at their smug faces, your excellencies. Completely unbecoming to young royals."

"We'll make sure they are punished, your royal highnesses." Lady Gertle shook her finger at the children. "Barley water soup for you three."

The King and Queen glanced at each other.

The Queen cleared her throat. "We appreciate your concern, Lady Gertle and Sir Gringle. However, the children received our absolute permission to leave the castle. We knew they were gone."

"What?" Sir Gringle's eyes bulged until Celeste worried they might pop right out of his face.

"Yes," the King waved his hand. "A fact you would have known if you'd chosen to tell us about the situation. Why didn't you inform us when you thought the children were missing?"

"Well, your graces," stammered Lady Gertle. "That is to say, we were only–"

"And as for barley-water soup," the Queen said in her most queenly manner. "the children will be dining with us this evening. They've been on a long journey, and they need real food."

"Yes." The King rubbed his beard. "From now on we wish to be notified before our children are punished for any reason so we can determine if the punishment is fair."

Lady Gertle open and closed her mouth like a giant fish, but didn't utter a word.

"After all," said the Queen, "we're their parents, aren't we?"

"Not to mention we're the royal rulers of the land," added the king.

Celeste, Torrin and Jude stood very still, not saying anything, until Lady Gertle and Sir Gringle walked out of the room, looking rather bewildered.

"And now, children, let's have dinner." The queen stretched her hands out to them. "Tell us all about your amazing adventures. From now on we promise to spend every dinner time as a family. Running the kingdom is not more important than spending time with you."

"That's right," said the King. "Tomorrow I shall write a proclamation. Barley-water soup shall be banished from the castle, henceforth and forever more."

Celeste snuggled by her mother's side, filled with so much happiness she could almost burst. But there was a question fluttering in her soul. Where would Aunt Maggie take them next?

THE END

Find Book 2 in the
Three Royal Children series,
*The Three Royal Children and the Purrflyer
Problem* on Amazon.com!
You can find out more about Angela Castillo's
books for kids at http://tobythetrilby.weebly.com

Did you enjoy *The Three Royal Children and the Batty Aunt*? You might like *The Amazing Adventures of Toby the Trilby*. Find it on Amazon! https://amzn.to/2RJAL5a

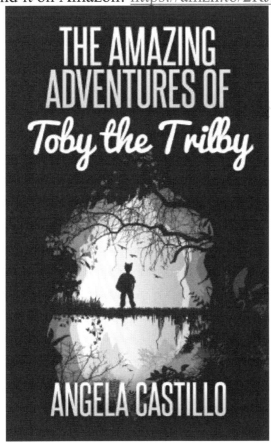

FAYETTE
— PRESS —

If you enjoyed *The Three Royal Children and the Batty Aunt*, you might also like these clean fantasy series (for teens and adults):

THE
SENTINEL TRILOGY

THE
STONES OF TERRENE

THE
UNDERWORLD MYTHOS

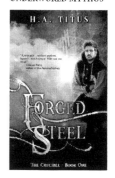

Blood-bonds with angels. Surreal mental abilities. Elemental gods. Maze Runner *meets* The Mortal Instruments *in this adrenaline-laced urban fantasy.*

Welcome to Terrene— where dragons exist, the past haunts, and magic is no myth. Welcome aboard the Sapphire.

Josh stumbled into the Underworld—rife with backstabbing fae and ancient powers—and he can't get out.

ABOUT THE AUTHOR

Angela Castillo loves living in the small town of
Bastrop Texas, and draws much of her writing inspiration
from life there. She loves to walk in the woods and
shop in the local stores. Castillo studied Practical Theology
and Music at Christ for the Nations in Dallas, Texas.
She was home-schooled all the way through high school and is the
oldest of seven kids. Castillo's greatest joys are her four children.

Printed in Great Britain
by Amazon